The Best School Day Ever

Written by Scott Peterson

Based on the series created by Dan Povenmire & Jeff "Swampy" Marsh

Printed in the United States of America   First Edition   1 3 5 7 9 10 8 6 4 2

ISBN 978-1-4231-3731-3

G658-7729-4-11135

For more Disney Press fun, visit www.disneybooks.com

DISNEY PRESS
NEW YORK

Yay, school!

"Okay, guys," Phineas and Ferb's mom suddenly called out. "Your sister, Candace, and I are going to the mall. Your dad is taking a nap, so try not to make too much noise."

After his mom and sister left, Phineas turned to Ferb and grinned. "I know what we're gonna do today," Phineas said, finishing his thought. "We're going to build our very own stunt school!"

A few minutes later, the gang had changed into safety gear and got right to work. Buford carried equipment while Isabella lined the yard with safety cones.

Meanwhile, Baljeet was at his desk waiting for class to start. "I get the feeling that this is not the kind of school I was hoping for," he said sadly.

First up was a classic stunt: the human cannonball. Baljeet was very nervous giving this stunt a try. But Buford fired the cannon before he could say no.

A few seconds later, Baljeet shot out of the cannon and landed with a giant thump. "I'm a stuntman," he mumbled.

This is awesome!

For their next lesson, Phineas explained how to do cool trapeze stunts.
"I knew you'd flip for this," Phineas told Isabella.

Perry the Platypus, also known as Agent P, had traveled to his secret headquarters to find out what evil plan Dr. Doofenshmirtz was plotting next.

But when he arrived, metal restraints snapped over his arms and trapped him! When he looked at the screen where Major Monogram usually appeared, he was shocked to see the face of Dr. Doofenshmirtz instead.

"Surprise!" Dr. Doofenshmirtz shouted. "I took over the spy agency with my newest invention—the Blow-'Em-Away-inator! I blew away some of the secret agents, and locked them in a bathroom at Paul Bunyan's Pancake Haus! I've warned the other agents to not even *try* to come near me. Now I will be able to *finally* take over the Tri-State Area!"

Agent P was able to quickly break free from his restraints. But suddenly trash fell out of the ceiling and his own chair tried to attack him!

Dr. Doofenshmirtz laughed from the monitor. He was controlling everything in the lair to harm Agent P!

"Now you're in trouble!" the doctor cackled.

But Dr. Doofenshmirtz was no match for Perry. The platypus escaped from the lair, hopped in his hover car, and sped away. The evil doctor climbed into his Blow-'Em-Away-inator and chased after him.

"All right, I'll follow you, Perry!" Dr. Doofenshmirtz shouted. "But once I blow you away, the Tri-State Area will be mine!"

Suddenly, Agent P heard a loud beeping. He looked down at his spy watch, where Major Monogram's face then appeared.

"Agent P, you've *got* to stay away from that -inator," he warned. "No one can recover from its high-powered winds... except maybe a stunt person."

Perry had an idea. He hoped it would work.

In the backyard, it was time for the stunt school final exam, an obstacle course full of challenges to test everyone's skills. Phineas explained that it would be difficult. But if they completed it, they would all be official stunt people!

Phineas started the course, with the rest of the gang following behind him. The first obstacle was triggered when a huge bucket of water overturned. The group skillfully jumped, flipped, and dived out of the way.

Next, cardboard cutouts of angry ninjas popped up all around them! Isabella, Buford, and Baljeet karate-kicked their opponents to the ground.

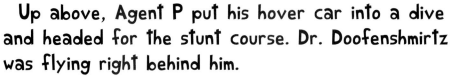

Up above, Agent P put his hover car into a dive and headed for the stunt course. Dr. Doofenshmirtz was flying right behind him.

"Come back here, Perry the Platypus!" he yelled.

"It sure is windy," Isabella commented, as powerful gusts blew through the course. Everyone managed to jump and leap out of the way. It was one of the toughest challenges yet!

"*Why* isn't my machine working?" Dr. Doofenshmirtz cried, as he noticed that everyone below was successfully dodging the winds from his -inator. Suddenly, Agent P jumped onto his back, causing the machine to spin and sputter. Then it started to blow the stunt school out of the backyard!

Agent P triggered his parachute and flew away. The -inator veered off in the other direction, dragging Dr. Doofenshmirtz along behind it.

Curse you, Perry the Platypus!

The wind had finally died down in Phineas and Ferb's backyard. Everyone had managed to successfully complete the obstacle course!

"Wow, I don't remember programming a giant windstorm," Phineas said. "Do you, Ferb? Well, anyway, we did it!"

"Congratulations!" Phineas cheered as he handed graduation caps and gowns to the group. "We're *officially* stunt people!" As the friends celebrated, Phineas and Ferb's mom and sister pulled into the driveway.

"How cute," their mom said. "They're playing school." Knowing her brothers all too well, Candace did *not* think it was cute. They were definitely up to something!

I'll get you next time, Phineas!

As everyone was about to head inside for a snack, a last gust of wind blew a cap on Perry, who had just arrived.

"Oh, there you are, Perry!" Phineas exclaimed. "Hey, you look good in a hat!"